This Book Belongs to:

Mickey's
Young Readers Library

VOLUME

9

Mickey
and the Big Storm

© MCMXC **The Walt Disney Company.**

Developed by The Walt Disney Company in conjunction with Nancy Hall, Inc.

Story by Mary Packard/Activities by Thoburn Educational Enterprises, Inc.

This book may not be reproduced or transmitted in any form or by any means.

ISBN 1-885222-42-4

Advance Publishers Inc., P.O. Box 2607, Winter Park, FL. 32790

Printed in the United States of America

0987654321

One cold winter day, Goofy and Mickey were visiting Donald.

"Shhh!" cried Goofy. "Did you hear that?"

Donald turned up the sound on his radio.

Mickey listened carefully.

"There will be at least one foot of snow," the voice said.

"Hurray!" Donald cried. "It's going to snow!"
"I'd better get going," said Mickey, as he put on
his coat. "I have to get ready for the storm."

Donald and Goofy looked at each other.

"We have to get ready for the storm, too," said Goofy.

"Right," agreed Donald. "We'll need a sled, of course."

"Then we can go sledding down Powder Hill!" Goofy said.

Goofy and Donald went to the garage to find the sled. Donald pulled it out from under a pile of boxes. Then he poked around some more.

"Look what I found," he said. He held up a pair of boots and some skis. "We might need these," he added, "in case the snow gets real deep."

"It's always best to be prepared," Goofy agreed.

"Boy-oh-boy-oh-boy!" Donald cried happily. "I can't believe it! It's snowing already!"

"I'd better get ready for the storm, too," said Goofy. "I'll see you tomorrow."

Goofy whistled a happy tune as he walked toward his house. He was thinking about all the fun he was going to have in the snow.

As soon as he got home, Goofy got all of his snow things together. He found his skis, his boots, and all of his warmest clothing. Then he piled them by the front door and went straight to bed.

Donald went to bed, too. "I hope the radio was right," Donald said, tucking himself in. "I hope it snows all night."

The next morning, Donald jumped out of bed bright and early. He raced over to the window.

"This is great!" he cried, looking out at the heavy blanket of snow. "It's still snowing! It's a good thing I'm prepared."

Donald got dressed and quickly found his sled.
He made his way down his snowy front walk, and
bumped smack into Goofy.

"I'm off to Powder Hill!" cried Donald. "Last one there is a rotten egg!"

Soon they were both at the top of the hill.

"Hang on!" shouted Donald.

Down, down, down they raced to the bottom of the hill.

"That was great!" cried Donald. He turned around to look at Goofy.

"Look out below!" came a voice, as a giant snowball came rolling down the hill. It came to a stop at Donald's feet.

Donald stared at the funny-looking snowball. It had a face like Goofy's!

"You just gave me a great idea!" Donald said, brushing the snow off his friend.

"Let's get everyone together for a snowball fight!"

"Okay," agreed Goofy, "as long as I don't have to be the snowball!"

"Very funny," said Donald. "Gee, the snow is coming down fast. Let's get the sled before we can't find it."

It wasn't long before Morty, Ferdie, Huey, Dewey, and Louie joined Donald and Goofy. They picked teams for the snowball fight. They built forts, and they made huge piles of snowballs. Finally it was time for the fight to begin.

"No fair, Goofy!" called Donald, when a snowball took him by surprise. "You're not supposed to hit the people on your own team."

"Gawrsh!" cried Goofy. "Was that you? It's snowing so hard I can't see very well."

By this time they had all been out in the snow for quite some time.

"We're going home now," said Huey, Dewey, and Louie. "We're fr-fr-fr-freezing!"

"Why don't we build a snowman?" asked Goofy.

"Okay," said Donald. "I'm getting tired of throwing snowballs anyway."

"Can we help?" asked Morty and Ferdie.

"Sure," replied Goofy. "Come on, we'll make a snowman together!"

With so many people helping, the snowman was finished in no time.

"That's the best-looking snowman I've ever seen," said Ferdie.

"I feel like a snowman!" said Morty. "It's really snowing hard and I'm cold! I think we should go home."

Ferdie agreed, and the two brothers left Goofy
and Donald to play in the deep snow.

After a few minutes, Goofy said, "Gawrsh, I'm
hungry!"

"Me, too!" said Donald. He thought for a
second. "There's only one thing to do," he said.
"Let's go home and make something to eat. Come
on, Goofy. You can come with me."

"I can't wait to get home," declared Donald.
Goofy agreed. "I sure could use a cup of hot
cocoa and a nice warm fire."

"Say no more," replied Donald. "Your wish is
about to come true. We're almost home."

But when they got to Donald's house, they were in for a few surprises.

"I'm out of firewood," groaned Donald. "I'll fix us some cocoa, though. That should warm us up."

"Uh-oh!" cried Donald, when he looked in his cupboard and refrigerator.

"I'm out of cocoa, and I'm out of milk. In fact, it looks like I'm out of just about everything!"

"Don't worry," replied Goofy. "We can always go to my house. I'm not exactly sure what I have in my cupboards. But I probably have more than you do."

It took them a long time to get to Goofy's house. The snow was very deep.

"It s-s-s-sure is c-c-c-cold!" chattered Donald.

But when they got to Goofy's house, it was cold inside, too. Goofy headed straight for the wood box.

"Gawrsh!" he cried. "I forgot to bring in the wood!"

Then Goofy looked in the kitchen. "I guess I forgot to go shopping, too!" He flipped on the light, but nothing happened.

"This is just great!" cried Donald. "We're out of firewood, food, and now we don't have any lights!"

"I know something else we're out of," said Goofy.

"Don't tell me," moaned Donald.

"We're out of luck," Goofy replied sadly.

"It's getting dark," said Donald. "We'll have to go into town. We need to buy some food and some candles."

So Goofy and Donald went out again. The snow was even deeper than before. It came all the way up to their knees!

"Hurray!" cried Goofy, when he saw the supermarket. "We're almost there."

But when they got to the door, they saw it was closed.

"Closed!" cried Donald. "They have some nerve! Let's try the corner grocery store. It's always open."

But the grocery store was closed too. And so was the delicatessen and the bakery.

"Everything's closed!" groaned Donald.

Just then the wind blew icy snow in his face.

"I'm cold, wet, and hungry!" moaned Donald.

"Me, too," said Goofy.

Goofy and Donald trudged through town. All they needed was to find *one* store that was open. But, of course, everyone had gone home because of the storm.

"What will we do now?" asked Goofy.

"Mickey will know what to do," answered Donald. "He's our only hope."

Goofy and Donald trudged up Mickey's neatly shoveled walk. Then they knocked on the door.

"Come in," cried Mickey. "What are you doing out on a night like this?"

Then Mickey got busy making his friends warm and comfortable.

Goofy and Donald sipped hot cocoa in front of the warm fire. They told Mickey about their day. "Gawrsh," Goofy asked, "why do you have plenty of food and firewood, Mickey?"

"Well, when I heard on the radio that there would be a storm, I decided to stop at the store on my way home to make sure I'd have everything I'd need. In fact, I'm extra prepared. Would you and Donald like to have dinner and spend the night?"

"We'd love to!" said Goofy and Donald.

"It looks like the only thing we did right to prepare for this storm was to have a good friend like you, Mickey." Donald smiled.

Think About It

Getting Snow-Ready

Which pictures show how Mickey got ready for the big snowstorm? Which ones show how Donald and Goofy got ready for the storm?

After your child does the activities in this book, refer to the *Young Readers Guide* for the answers to these activities and for additional games, activities, and ideas.

What Would You Do?

Imagine what would happen if a big snowstorm came to your town. How would you get ready?

What would you do that was different from how Donald and Goofy prepared for the storm? What would you do that was the same? What would you do that was different from what Mickey did? What would you do that was the same?

Fun With Words

Snow-Words Jumble

Help Goofy figure out the jumbled snow words below. (Hint: Use the words in the clue box to help you.)

SNLLBAOWS
KISS   STEAKS
ANMWONS   DELS
FKLEANOWSS

SNOWBALLS	SKATES	SLED
SKIS	SNOWMAN	SNOWFLAKES

Winter Word Search

Find the five winter words hidden in the word search. (Hint: The words in the clue box can be found from left to right and top to bottom.)

SNOW	SKATES	SKIS	ICE	SLED

S N O W X Y Z R

K S K I S B X W

A I C E R T C B

T U R V X B T D

E B J G H V K L

S L E D T P R V

Mickey's Young Readers Library • Mickey's Young Readers Library
Readers Library • Mickey's Young Readers Library • Mickey's Young
Mickey's Young Readers Library • Mickey